Designed by Flowerpot Press in Franklin, TN.
www.FlowerpotPress.com
Designer: Jonas Fearon Bell
Editor: Katrine Crow
ROR-0808-0111
ISBN: 978-1-4867-1265-6
Made in China/Fabriqué en Chine

The wheels on the bus go **round** and **round**,
round and **round**, **round** and **round**.
The wheels on the bus go **round** and **round**,
all through the town.

The puddles on the road go splash splash splash,
splash splash splash, splash splash splash.
The puddles on the road go splash splash splash,
all through the town.

The wipers on the bus go swish swish swish,

swish swish swish, swish swish swish.

The wipers on the bus go swish swish swish,

all through the town.

Bump

The horn on the bus goes beep beep beep,

beep beep beep, beep beep beep.

The horn on the bus goes beep beep beep,

all through the town.

The people on the bus go **back** and **forth**,
back and **forth**, **back** and **forth**.
The people on the bus go **back** and **forth**,
all through the town.

The people on the bus go **up** and **down**,
up and **down**, **up** and **down**.
The people on the bus go **up** and **down**,
all through the town.

The kids on the bus go blah blah blah,
blah blah blah, blah blah blah.

The kids on the bus go **blah blah blah**,
all through the town.

The driver on the bus goes shhh shhh shhh,
shhh shhh shhh, shhh shhh shhh.

The driver on the bus goes shhh shhh shhh,
all through the town.

The kids on the bus say, "Thanks for the ride!
Thanks for the ride! Thanks for the ride!"
The kids on the bus say, "Thanks for the ride!"
and now they're all at school.